Air Power

V-22 OSPREY

MEGAN COOLEY PETERSON

BLACK RABBIT BOOKS

Bolt is published by Black Rabbit Books
P.O. Box 3263, Mankato, Minnesota, 56002.
www.blackrabbitbooks.com

Jennifer Besel, editor; Grant Gould & Michael Sellner, designers; Omay Ayres, photo researcher

Library of Congress Cataloging-in-Publication Data
Names: Peterson, Megan Cooley, author.
Title: V-22 Osprey / by Megan Cooley Peterson.
Description: Mankato, Minnesota : Black Rabbit Books, [2019] | Series: Bolt. Air power | Includes bibliographical references and index. | Audience: Grades 4-6. | Audience: Ages 9-12.
Identifiers: LCCN 2017027161 (print) | LCCN 2017027644 (ebook) | ISBN 9781680725025 (ebook) | ISBN 9781680723861 (library binding) | ISBN 9781680726800 (paperback)
Subjects: LCSH: V-22 Osprey (Transport plane)—Juvenile literature. | Transport planes—United States—Juvenile literature.
Classification: LCC UG1242.T7 (ebook) | LCC UG1242.T7 P47 2019 (print) | DDC 358.4/483—dc23
LC record available at https://lccn.loc.gov/2017027161

Printed in China. 3/18

Image Credits

Alamy: 508 collection, Cover; Domenico Cicchetti, 28 (b); Mint Photography, 20–21; PJF Military Collection, 3, 19 (b), 28 (t); RGB Ventures / SuperStock, 25; US Marines Photo, 24 (r); Z2A1, 19 (t); ZUMA Press, 22; commons.wikimedia.org: 15 (line drawings); PFC E. E. Green, U.S. Army, 9; US Marine Corps/Gunnery Sgt. Bill Lisbon, 4–5; US Navy/Paul Farley, 12 (t); defense.gov, US Air Force/Tech. Sgt. Charles Larkin Sr., U.S. Air Force, 6; Dreamstime: Brett Critchley, 16–17; hu.wikipedia.org: 13 (t); marines.mil/: US Marine Corps/Lance Cpl. Eric Clayton, 10–11; navair.navy.mil: US Marines Photo, 26–27; navy.mil: US Navy, 12 (b); Shutterstock: Handatko, 24 (gauge); inspired-fiona, 15 (bkgd); Santiparp Wattanaporn, 12–13 (bkgd); SpaceKris, 1; Thor Jorgen Udvang, 31; WorldStock, 32; ymphotos, 23; usafe.af.mil: US Air Force/Tech. Sgt. Chrissy Bes, 13 (b)

CONTENTS

CHAPTER 1

A Daring RESCUE

In 2011, a fighter jet flew over Libya. Suddenly, something inside the plane broke. The plane crashed to the ground. The pilot lived. But he was trapped in enemy **territory**.

U.S. Marines boarded two V-22 Osprey helicopters. They had to move fast to save the pilot.

USAF
0041

Sneaking Past the Enemy

The Ospreys flew into action. One landed near the pilot. Marines quickly got him inside the chopper. Then they lifted off. The enemy had no idea the Ospreys had been there.

An osprey is a bird of prey. The chopper is named after this bird.

CHAPTER 2

HISTORY of the V-22 Osprey

The U.S. military has flown helicopters since the 1940s. Their **vertical** takeoff and landing is great for missions. But helicopters can't fly as fast as airplanes. They also can't go as far. The military needed a new kind of aircraft.

U.S. ARMY

The Osprey seats up to 24 people. The seating is good for rescue missions.

Unusual Aircraft

Engineers created an unusual aircraft. The V-22 Osprey is part airplane and part helicopter. It **hovers** like a helicopter. It has the speed of an airplane.

V-22 OSPREY TIMELINE

March 1989
Osprey takes first flight.

May 1988
Osprey is shown to the public.

1980

1981
The U.S. Department of Defense starts a program to make aircraft with vertical takeoff.

2005
Marines get first fleet of MV-22s.

2010

2006
Air Force gets first fleet of CV-22s.

2007
Ospreys fly in Iraq War.

CHAPTER 3

The V-22 Osprey FEATURES

The Osprey is an amazing machine. Its tilt **rotors** move even when the craft is flying. With the rotors up, pilots can take off vertically. Then they can face the rotors forward. The craft zooms off like a plane.

V-22 OSPREY STATS

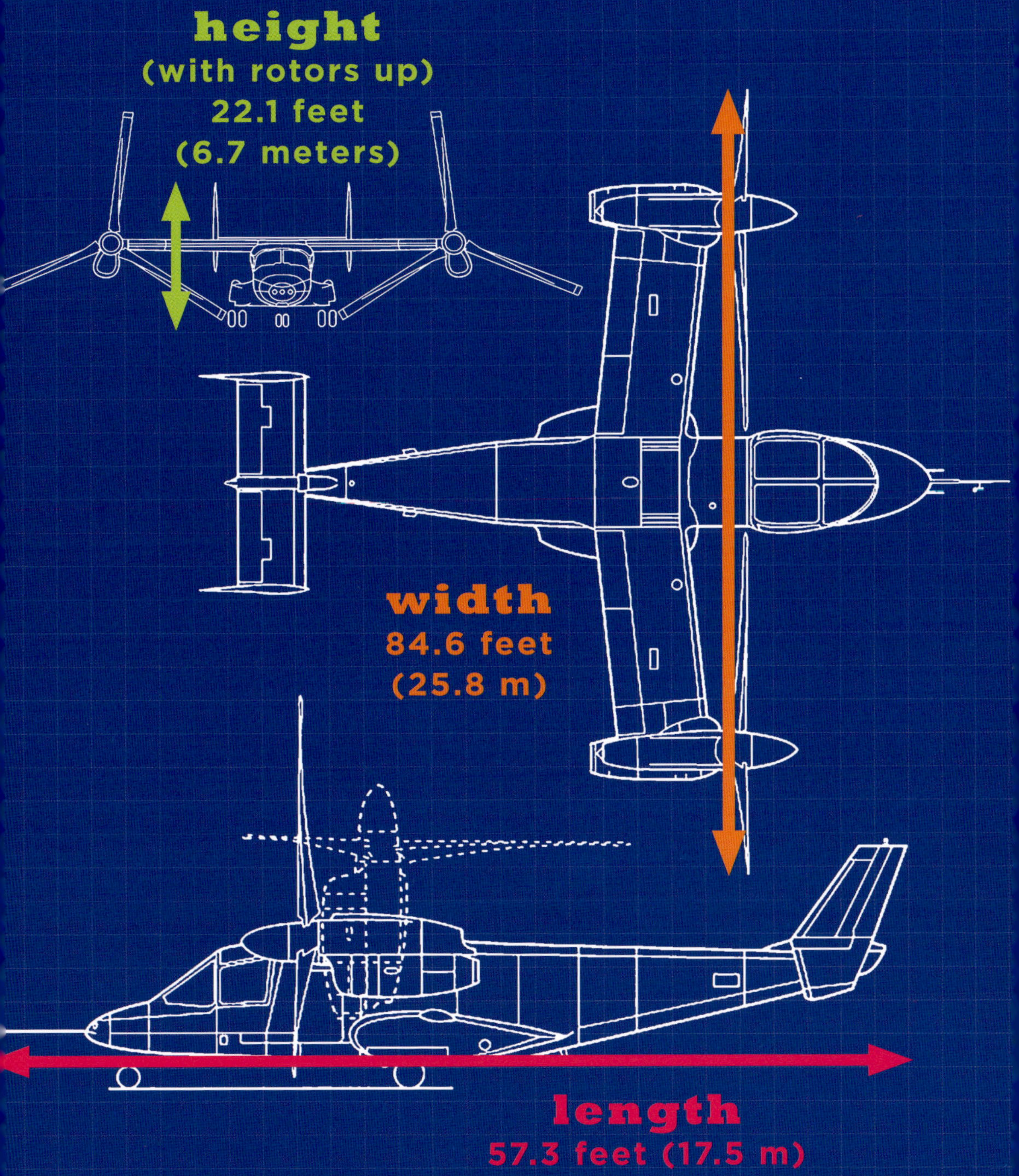

COMPARING MILITARY HELICOPTER TOP SPEEDS

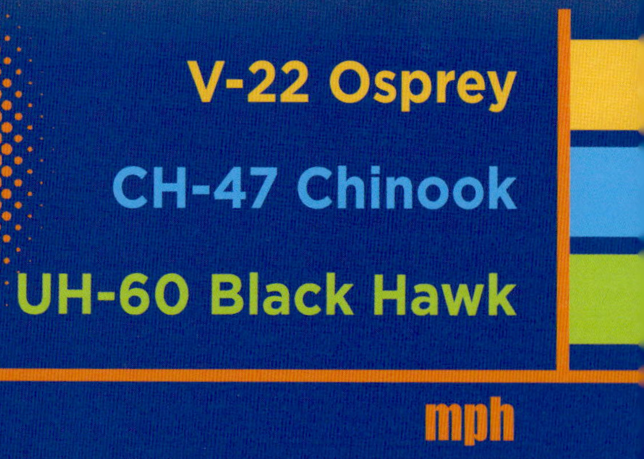

Fantastic Speed

The Osprey rules the sky. It flies up to 363 miles (584 kilometers) per hour. That speed is faster than any other military helicopter.

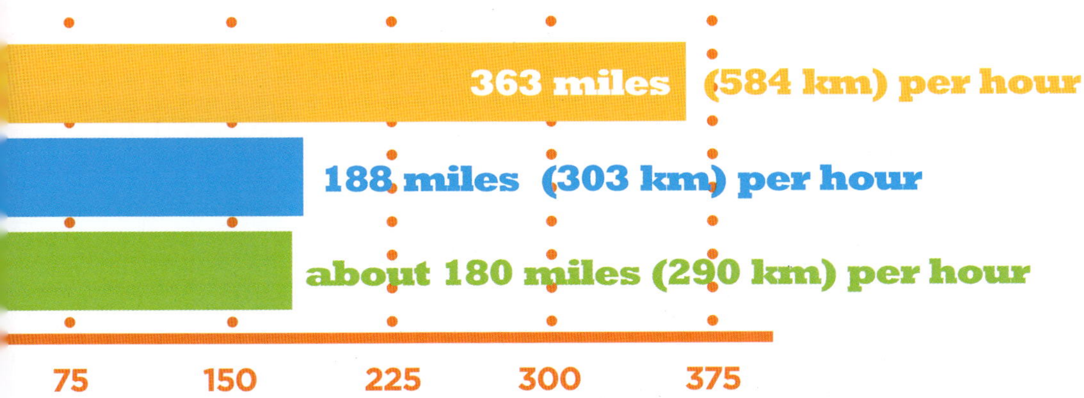

Two Kinds

The U.S. military uses two types of Ospreys. Marines fly the MV-22 during rescues. They also use them to move soldiers and supplies.

The Air Force flies the CV-22. They use it for long-distance secret rescues.

MV-22	vs.	CV-22
2	cockpit crew seating	3
1,721 gallons (6,515 liters)	fuel capacity	2,025 gallons (7,665 L)
$71.92 million	cost per aircraft	$69.22 million

V-22 OSPREY PARTS

COCKPIT
MACHINE GUN

CHAPTER 4

The Osprey in ACTION

In 2013, a **typhoon** hit the Philippines. Huge waves washed away villages. The people there needed help. The U.S. military used Ospreys to bring supplies. Ospreys and other aircraft brought more than 66,000 pounds (29,937 kilograms) of supplies in 24 hours.

BY THE NUMBERS

493 MILES
(793 KM)
MAXIMUM DISTANCE WITHOUT REFUELING

397
revolutions per minute

MAXIMUM ROTOR SPEED

52,600 POUNDS
(23,859 kg)
MAXIMUM VERTICAL TAKEOFF WEIGHT
24,000 FEET (7,315 m)
MAXIMUM CRUISING HEIGHT

Risky Mission

Ospreys had a tricky mission in 2009. Soldiers had to remove a **terrorist** leader in Afghanistan. The choppers had to land in daylight. No problem! They landed in secret. Marines captured the leader in less than 5 minutes.

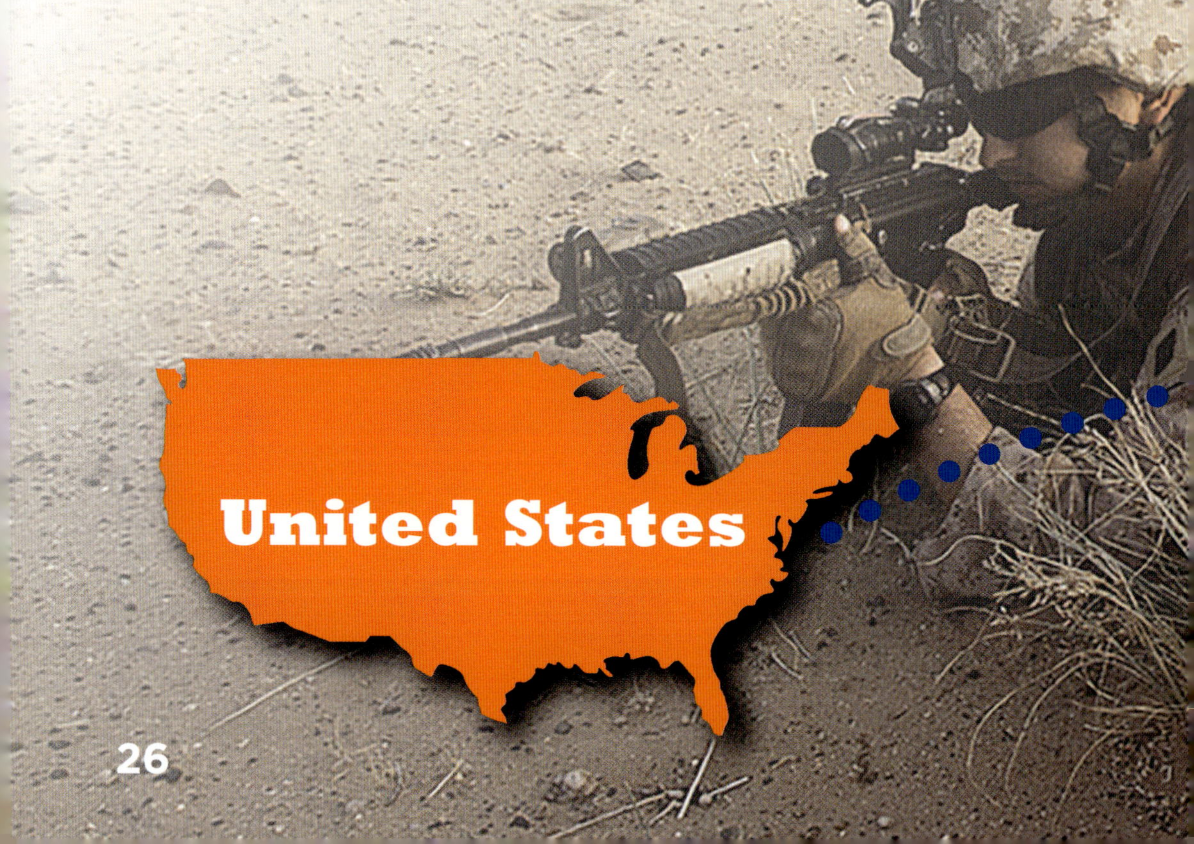

The country of Japan has also purchased Ospreys.

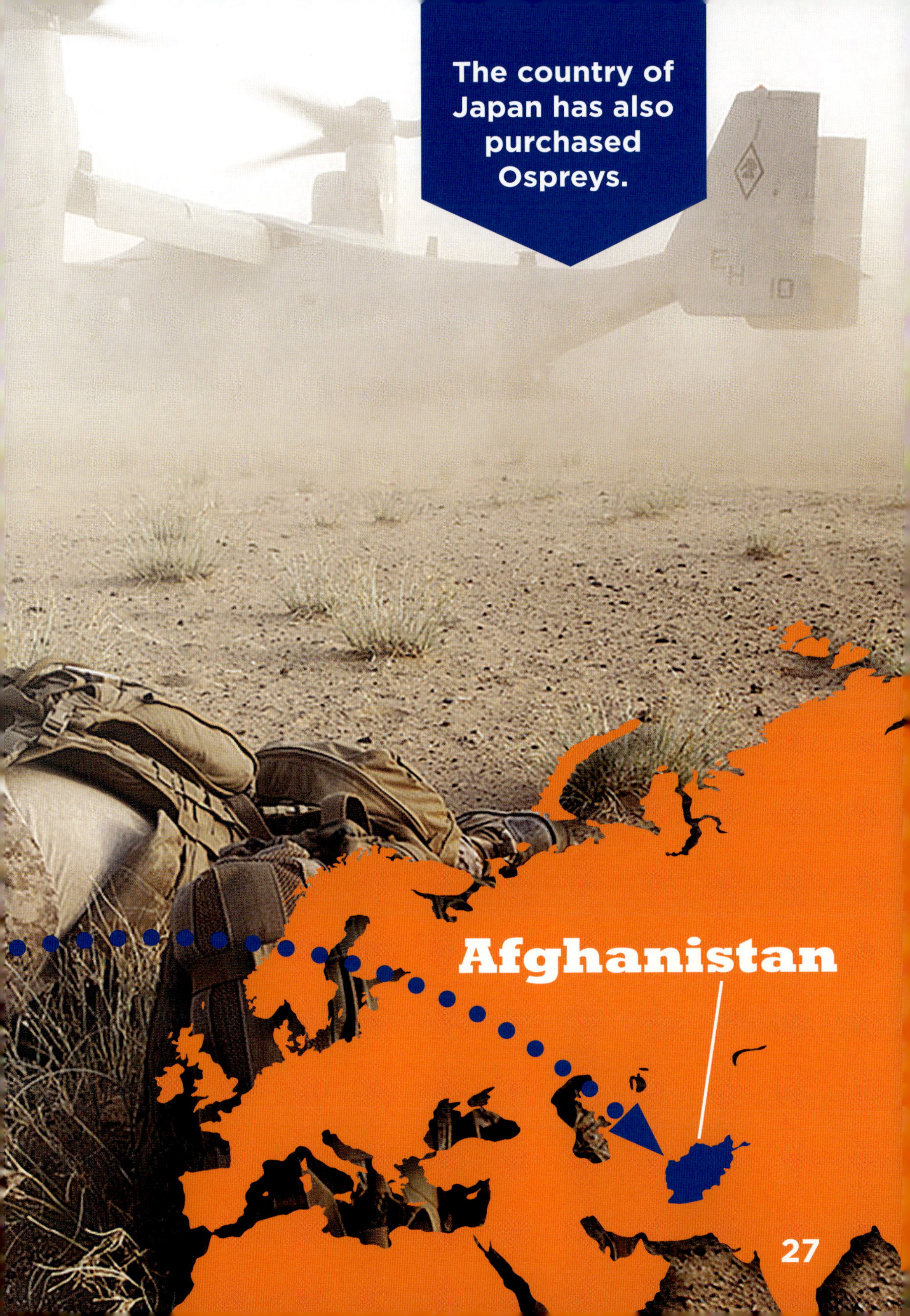

The chopper's rotors fold up. This action makes it easier to store the large aircraft.

Powerful Aircraft

The Osprey is an amazing aircraft. It moves like a helicopter. It has the speed of an airplane. The Osprey is always ready to help.

GLOSSARY

engineer (en-juh-NEER)—a designer or builder

hover (HUHV-er)—floating in the air without moving any direction

revolution (rev-uh-LOO-shun)—a single complete turn

rotor (RO-tuhr)—spinning blades that support a helicopter in the air

territory (TER-uh-tor-ee)—a geographic area belonging to or under the control of a governmental authority

terrorist (TER-ur-ist)—a person who uses violent acts to frighten people in order to achieve a goal

typhoon (ty-FOON)—a hurricane that happens in the region of the Philippines or the China Sea

vertical (VUR-tuh-kuhl)—straight up and down

BOOKS

Garstecki, Julia. *Military Aircraft.* Military Tech. Mankato, MN: Black Rabbit Books, 2018.

Harrison, Paul. *Supercopters.* Mean Machines. London: Arcturus, 2015.

Nagelhout, Ryan. *Military Helicopters.* Mighty Military Machines. New York: Gareth Stevens Publishing, 2015.

WEBSITES

Bell Boeing V-22 Osprey
www.bellhelicopter.com/en/military/bell-boeing-v-22/

Boeing: V-22 Osprey
www.boeing.com/defense/v-22-osprey/

CV-22 Osprey
www.af.mil/AboutUs/FactSheets/Display/tabid/224/Article/104531/cv-22-osprey.aspx

INDEX